Not Me!

Not Me!

Valeri Gorbachev

I Like to Read®

Holiday House / New York

"I like the beach," said Bear.
"Not me!" said Chipmunk.

"I like the sun," said Bear.
"Not me!" said Chipmunk.

"It is hot!" said Bear.
"I will dive in."
"Not me!" said Chipmunk.

"I like to swim," said Bear.
"Not me!" said Chipmunk.

"I am not a beach person,"
said Chipmunk.

"Now I will play ball," said Bear.
"Not me!" said Chipmunk.

"I see a cute little fish,"
said Bear.
"Not me!"
said Chipmunk.

"I hope
we see a big fish,"
said Bear.

"Not me!" said Chipmunk.

"Why did you come?" said Bear.
"I came to be with you,"
said Chipmunk.

"You are a good friend,"
said Bear.
"That's me!" said Chipmunk.

To my grandson Avigdor

I LIKE TO READ is a registered trademark of Holiday House, Inc.
Copyright © 2016 by Valeri Gorbachev
All Rights Reserved
HOLIDAY HOUSE is registered in the U.S. Patent and Trademark Office.
Printed and Bound in November 2015 at Tien Wah Press, Johor Bahru, Johor, Malaysia.
The artwork was created with watercolor and ink.
www.holidayhouse.com
First Edition
1 3 5 7 9 10 8 6 4 2

Library of Congress Cataloging-in-Publication Data
Gorbachev, Valeri, author, illustrator.
Not me! / Valeri Gorbachev. — First edition.
pages cm
Summary: While Bear enjoys a day at the beach, Chipmunk,
who is not a beach person, does not, suffering one mishap after another all in the interests
of spending time with his good friend Bear.
ISBN 978-0-8234-3546-3 (hardcover)
[1. Beaches—Fiction. 2. Friendship—Fiction.
3. Bears—Fiction. 4. Chipmunks—Fiction.] I. Title.
PZ7.G6475No 2016
[E]—dc23
2015019726
ISBN 978-0-8234-3547-0 (paperback)

You will like these too!

Come Back, Ben by Ann Hassett and John Hassett
A *Kirkus Reviews* Best Book

Dinosaurs Don't, Dinosaurs Do by Steve Björkman
A Notable Social Studies Trade Book for Young People
An IRA/CBC Children's Choice

Fish Had a Wish by Michael Garland
A *Kirkus Reviews* Best Book
A Top 25 Children's Books list book

The Fly Flew In by David Catrow
An IRA/CBC Children's Choice
Maryland Blue Crab Young Reader Award Winner

Look! by Ted Lewin
The Correll Book Award for Excellence
in Early Childhood Informational Text

Me Too! by Valeri Gorbachev
A Bank Street Best Children's Book of the Year

Mice on Ice by Rebecca Emberley and Ed Emberley
A Bank Street Best Children's Book of the Year
An IRA/CBC Children's Choice

Pig Has a Plan by Ethan Long
An IRA/CBC Children's Choice

See Me Dig by Paul Meisel
A *Kirkus Reviews* Best Book

See Me Run by Paul Meisel
A Theodor Seuss Geisel Award Honor Book
An ALA Notable Children's Book

You Can Do It! by Betsy Lewin
A Bank Street Best Children's Book of the Year,
Outstanding Merit

See more I Like to Read® books.
Go to www.holidayhouse.com/I-Like-to-Read/

Some More I Like to Read® Books in Paperback

Animals Work by Ted Lewin

Bad Dog by David McPhail

Big Cat by Ethan Long

Can You See Me? by Ted Lewin

Cat Got a Lot by Steve Henry

Drew the Screw by Mattia Cerato

The Fly Flew In by David Catrow

Happy Cat by Steve Henry

Here Is Big Bunny by Steve Henry

I Have a Garden by Bob Barner

I See and See by Ted Lewin

Little Ducks Go by Emily Arnold McCully

Me Too! by Valeri Gorbachev

Mice on Ice by Rebecca Emberley and Ed Emberley

Not Me! by Valeri Gorbachev

Pig Has a Plan by Ethan Long

Pig Is Big on Books by Douglas Florian

What Am I? Where Am I? by Ted Lewin

You Can Do It! by Betsy Lewin

Visit http://www.holidayhouse.com/I-Like-to-Read/ for more
about I Like to Read® books, including flash cards, reproducibles
and the complete list of titles.

"I like the beach," said Bear.
"Not me!" said Chipmunk.
But he went.

Valeri Gorbachev
likes to read and draw.
And he likes to make
books for children.

ISBN 978-0-8234-3547-0
50699

0408
GRL D

HOLIDAY HOUSE, INC.
www.holidayhouse.com

EAN
9 780823 435470